HUMMY
AND THE WAX CASTLE

Author

Elizabeth Ernst

Illustrator

Steve Pitstick

Institute for Creation Research
Santee, California

HUMMY AND THE WAX CASTLE

Published, produced and distributed by the **INSTITUTE FOR CREATION RESEARCH**

Richard B. Bliss, Ed.D., Project Director

CONSULTANTS
Theodore Fischbacher, Education, Ph.D.
Jean Sloat Morton, Biology, Ph.D.
Gary E. Parker, Biology, Ed.D.
Hazel May Rue, Education, M.S.
Harold S. Slusher, Physics, M.S., D.Sc.,Ph.D.

CONTRIBUTING TEAM MEMBERS

ILLUSTRATORS
Shirlene Barrett, Jonathan Chong, Richard Holt, Doug Jennings, Karen Myers, Steve Pitstick, Marvin Ross, Barbara Sauer, Sandy Thornton, Linda Vance, Jay Wegter, Frankie Winn, Tim Lindquist, Ron Fisher, Jeanie Elliott

PROJECT WRITING STAFF

Deborah Bainer—Malaysia
Anne Beams—Germany
Gary G. Eastman—California
Elizabeth Ernst—Oregon
Kenneth F. Ernst, Jr.—Oregon
Olive Fischbacher—California
Norman Fox—Oregon
Virginia Gray Hastings—Illinois
Marilyn F. Hallman—Texas
Alberta Hanson—California
Deborah Hayes—Texas

Richard Holt—Iowa
Melody J. McIntyre—Pennsylvania
Fred Pauling—Virginia
Hazel May Rue—Oregon
Barbara Sauer—Illinois
Janice Sherwin—California
Wilburn Sooter—Washington
Ivan Stonehocker—Canada
Harold C. Watkins—California
Susan E. Watkins—California
Fred Willson—California

HUMMY AND THE WAX CASTLE

Copyright © 1984, 2nd ed. 1997
Revised 1997
Institute for Creation Research
P.O. Box 2667
El Cajon, California 92021

Library of Congress Catalog Card Number 84-80074

ISBN 0-932766-14-5

Cataloging in Publication Data

Ernst, Elizabeth
  Hummy and the Wax Castle / author, Elizabeth Ernst /
illustrator, Steve Pitstick

  For elementary grades.
  1. Bees—Juvenile literature.
I. Title. II. Pitstick, Steve.
      595.799

To The Reader

Have you ever watched a honeybee at work? Did you know that a bee lives in a castle—made of wax? Do you know which bees do different jobs? Come with Josh as he meets Hummy and learns exciting facts about bees. Discover what life is like in a wax castle!

God wants us to explore His creation. He is pleased when we marvel at the special parts of His plan for life. Turn the page and read about some things that you've never known.

Pronunciation Key

The following pronunciation key is based on the Thorndike-Barnhart School Dictionary. These markings are used in a glossary to help you pronounce the important bold-faced words used in the story.

hat, āge, fär
let, ēqual, térm
it, īce
hot, ōpen, ôrder, oil, out
cup, put, rüle
ch, child
ng long
sh, she
th, thin
Ŧh, then
zh, measure
uh represents *a* in about, *e* in taken, *i* in pencil,
      o in lemon, *u* in circus

Contents

Chapter 1

A Teeny Tiny Friend

For weeks Josh had looked forward to summer vacation. He had ridden his bike to all of his favorite spots. He had played with every game he owned. He had read every book he had borrowed, and he longed to go to the library for more. Now the thrill of summer vacation was wearing off.

Josh slumped in his chair and whined, "What is there to do?"

Josh's mother put the last batch of honey bars in the oven. "Josh, what you need is something new," she said. "Your teacher told me that you are very good at writing and explaining things. Go out and watch the bees in the tree behind the house. See what you can learn, but be careful! Don't get stung!"

"Okay!" Josh agreed. He liked being outdoors, and he loved nature. Studying living things was his favorite part about science. He asked, "Then may we go to the library this afternoon? We could check out some books on bees."

"Sure," his mother replied. She saw Josh look longingly at his favorite snack cooling on the counter. "Help yourself to some honey bars, Son," she offered.

"Thanks!" Josh cried. He picked up a handful of honey bars and went to get his magnifying glass, binoculars, and sunglasses. The door slammed behind him as he ran outside.

Josh headed straight for the clover field behind their house. That was where his dad had discovered a hive in a big tree. Josh knew that summer is the busiest time of the year for bees. He didn't worry about being stung. He knew that he didn't get as sick from bee stings as some of his friends did. Josh also remembered that his father told him that often the bees are too busy, on warm days, to show much interest in people. He would be careful, though, and not bother the bees.

The sun's warmth felt good on his back, and Josh whistled as he walked quickly across the clover field. As he neared the old tree, he spotted the beehive.

Josh lay down in a shady spot under the tree and lazily munched the last of the honey bars. He watched the busy honeybees as they came and went. Their pleasant buzzing noise, the warm afternoon, and his full stomach made Josh feel very sleepy.

Bzz, bzz, buzz-zzz. One honeybee zoomed near Josh. "Good morning!"

Josh sleepily turned his head. Someone had spoken to him, but there was no one there. Was he dreaming?

The honeybee settled on Josh's shoulder. "Good morning!" the bee repeated.

Josh was so surprised, he didn't even try to run away. He looked more closely at the bee. "D-Did you talk to me?" he asked.

"Yes. I can tell there's honey in your snack. Would you like to know where honey comes from? I'd be glad to tell you about my life."

Josh couldn't believe his ears! Could he be talking to a bee? "Sure!" he replied excitedly. "Go ahead."

"My name is Hummy. I am a **worker bee**, I live in the hive with other **worker bees**, a **queen bee**, and some **drones**. Worker bees and queen bees are female. Drones are male. If you look closely, you can see how differently we are all made. The queen is the biggest bee, the drone bees are the next largest, and worker bees like me are the smallest."

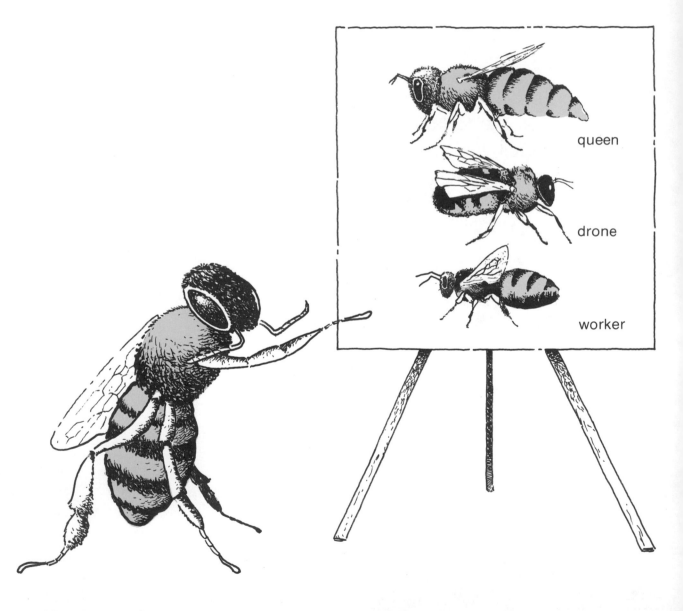

queen

drone

worker

Chapter 2

Josh Takes a Closer Look

Josh held out his hand, and Hummy flew down and landed on it. Josh found that studying a bee is really interesting. "You sure are tiny! You don't weigh much, either," Josh exclaimed.

"No, we don't. One reason is that bees don't have bones. Our skin is the only skeleton we have. Without it we would be soft and helpless."

Josh picked up his magnifying glass. He looked carefully at the sides of the bee. He could see some tiny round circles. "Hummy, why do you need these holes?" Josh asked.

"I breathe through these holes. They are called **spiracles**," Hummy said. "I wasn't created with a nose, and I don't have ears like you do, Josh, but I do feel **vibrations**. I can feel when something is close to me."

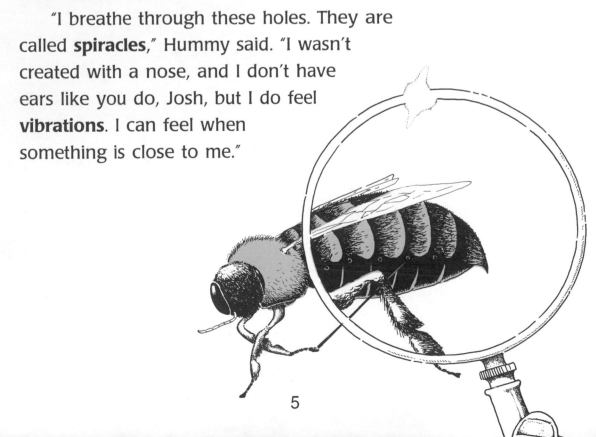

"Where is your mouth?" Josh questioned.

"I have a tongue, which is a long tube. I suck water, **nectar**, and honey with it, just like people drink through a straw," Hummy explained.

Smiling, Josh thought about having a straw for a tongue. "Can you move your tongue?" he asked.

"I sure can! I can move it in all directions," Hummy said. "Say, Josh, if you had a microscope, you could learn even more about me. You could see different cells."

"We talked about cells in school this year," Josh said. "I remember that some cells are shaped like boxes, and some are like pancakes. Others are like footballs, and many are like lumpy basketballs."

"Good for you, Josh! Do you know how cells work?" Hummy asked.

"Yes! The cell needs energy to do its work. This energy comes from foods with sugars and fats," Josh said. "Oh! I remember something else. A **muscle** cell pulls, a **nerve** cell sends messages, and a **gland** cell makes **chemicals**."

muscle

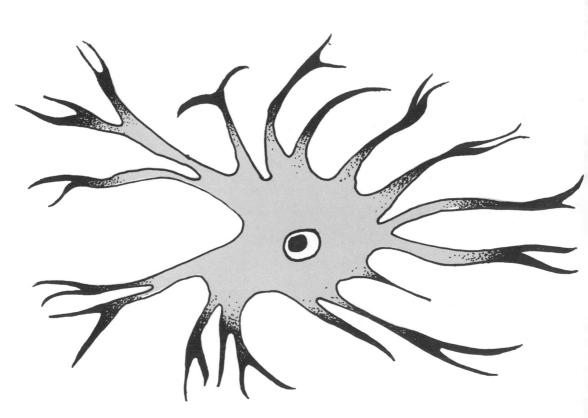

nerve

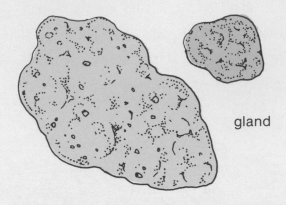

gland

As Josh thought about the cell, he realized how perfectly all these cells were made to do their job.

Hummy buzzed loudly, "You are a good student, Josh. Do you remember the name of the special code that gives the plan, telling the cell what it is going to be?"

"That's easy!" Josh boasted proudly. "It's **DNA!**"

"Very good, Josh. The special cell that becomes a bee, like me, contains all the plans for me. No other creature has plans like these. These plans are for my size, shape, color, and my way of life."

"You are an insect, aren't you?" asked Josh, as he continued to look at the little bee.

"Yes, and I am a honeybee. I am like a chemical factory that is divided into three parts. My head is the main office where big decisions are made. My **thorax** is the motor room. My **abdomen** is the storeroom."

8

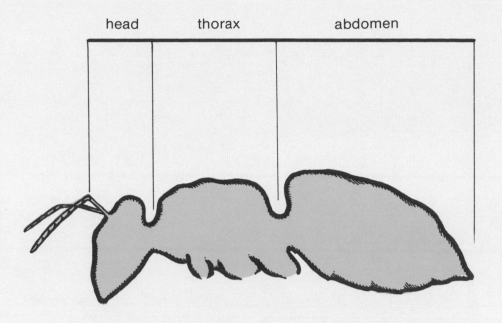

head   thorax   abdomen

"Wow! You are very special! It seems like someone carefully planned everything about you," Josh exclaimed. "I wonder, though . . . I read in a book that bees changed from a simple creature to the more **complex** insect that you are now. Could this really happen?"

"That is something to think about, Josh," Hummy said. "I think I will show you some of my complex parts and you can see that I'm not a simple creature at all."

Josh was eager to learn more.

Chapter 3

Head First

"Tell me about your eyes. They don't look at all like mine," Josh said.

"Well, let's see . . ." Hummy paused for a moment. "I have three small 'simple' eyes in a triangle at the top of my head. There are also large eyes on each side of my head. They are called compound eyes." Hummy explained. "Each compound eye is made of thousands of smaller eyes crowded together."

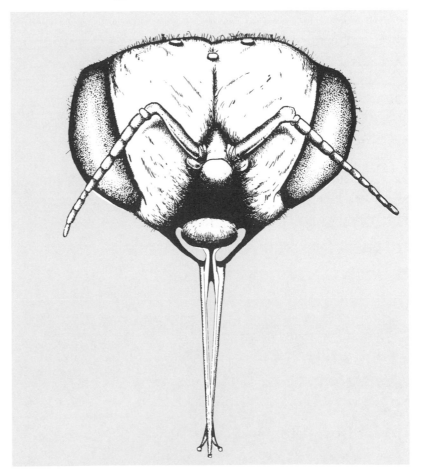

"Amazing! With all of those eyes, you must see a lot of things," Josh exclaimed.

"I can see how things are alike and different. I can see moving things best." Hummy laughed, "I bet I can do something you can't do—I can sleep with my eyes open."

"You are SOME bee!" Josh said, as he put on his sunglasses. "Hummy, is it true that you can see something called **ultraviolet rays**? Even with my sunglasses on, I can't see any special rays."

"People cannot see ultraviolet rays," Hummy explained, "but bees can! I can use the sun even on a cloudy day. I use the ultraviolet rays that come through the clouds to find my directions. The rays are like pathways. My eyes were created so complex that even I can't understand everything about them."

"What else can you tell me about your eyes?" Josh questioned.

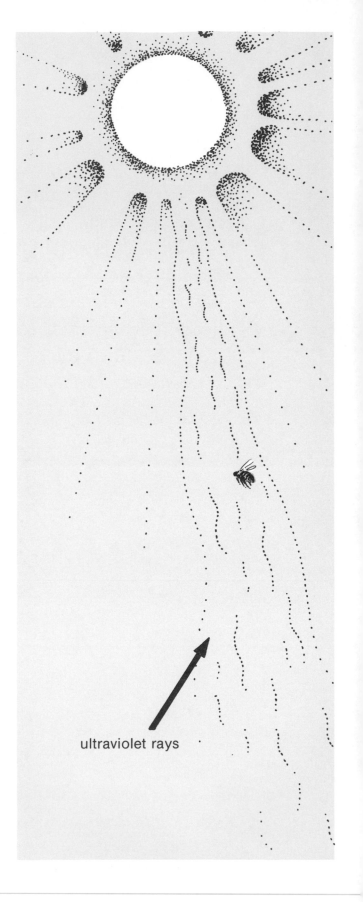

ultraviolet rays

"I have many **lenses**. In fact, I have so many, I can see in all directions at once. Since light is made up of many parts, the sky looks like a colored map to me. I know where I am going when I see my sky map."

"Do you see colors the same way that I do?" Josh wanted to know.

"No, for one thing, I can't see the color red. I don't see things as you do."

Hummy continued, "Do you see that flower over there? It looks like a checkerboard to me."

"You're right," said Josh. "I don't see it like that."

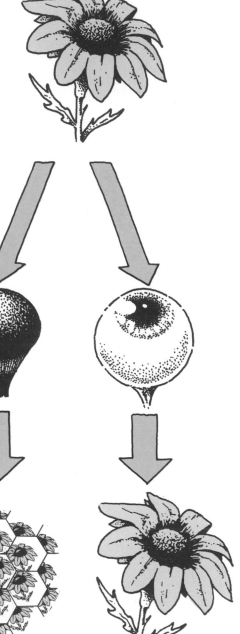

Josh continued to study his small friend. "Hummy, are those things sticking out of your head called **antennae** or feelers?"

"You can call them by either name," answered Hummy. "Each antennae is divided into two parts by a **hinge**. The antennae, or feelers, are fastened to the front of my head by special joints. I am always using them for smelling and touching."

"I wish I had antennae on my head," Josh said jokingly, "but my head is so different." Then Josh noticed something else. "Your head is shaped like a heart. Are all bees' heads shaped like that?"

"First of all, we who are workers are a different shape and size from the queen and the drones," Hummy informed Josh proudly.

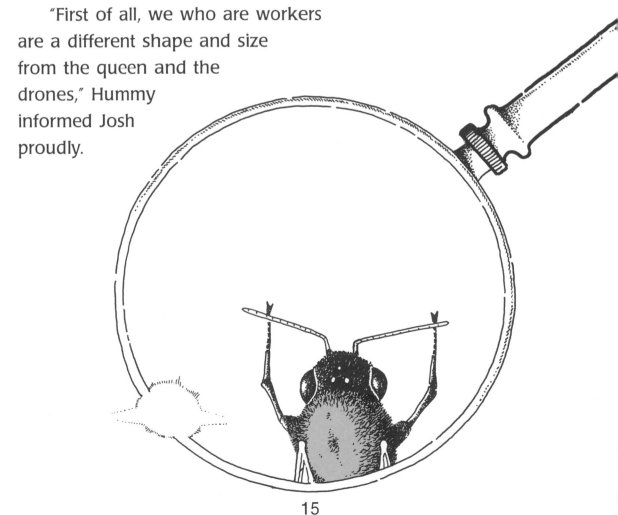

15

"Our heads don't look alike. As you said, my head is heart-shaped, just like other workers. A drone's head is almost round. The queen's face looks like mine, but my brain is larger.

Hummy paused for a moment and then continued. "We are different in other ways, too. The queen is quite long. Her wings only reach half way along her abdomen. She also has long legs. The drones weigh about the same as the queen. They have very long wings that completely cover their abdomen." Hummy lifted her wings and allowed Josh to study their shape and size before she refolded them neatly. "I am the smallest of the three kinds of bees. I weigh only half as much as the queen or drones. My body is designed to help me do my work. My wings don't cover my abdomen. My mouth is especially made to mold wax. My third pair of legs are designed to carry pollen loads. My tongue is long so I can gather nectar and pollen."

Josh smiled. "You must keep your slim, trim shape by working so hard."

"I do work hard," Hummy agreed, "but I enjoy doing what I have been designed to do!"

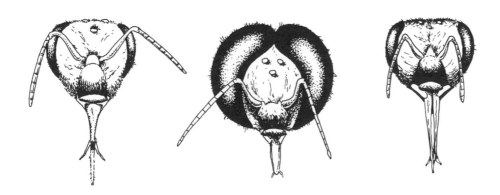

Chapter 4

Super Bee!

Josh leaned against the tree.   "I know quite a bit about your head, antennae, and eyes, but what about the rest of your body?" he asked.

Hummy flew from Josh's shoulder to a clover blossom. She gathered a lot of colored flower dust on her back legs. Hummy buzzed her answer loudly back to Josh.

"I have three legs on each side of my **thorax** or 'motor room.' I use them to walk and to work. Watch me brush this pollen off my body."

Josh knelt on the ground and looked at Hummy more closely. "It looks like you have baskets on your hind legs," said Josh, watching his friend move from one blossom to another.

"Yes, those are **pollen baskets** on the outside of my back legs," Hummy told Josh.

"Isn't that a big load for a little bee? You must be very strong!" Josh said in amazement.

"Yes, my leg muscles are really strong. I can pull 300 times my own weight. Josh, if you weighed 80 pounds and could pull 300 times your own weight, how much could you pull?"

Josh thought. "Uh, I guess I would multiply 80 times 300. Let's see . . ." said Josh, figuring the problem in his head, "that would be 24,000 pounds, 12 tons! Wow-ee! Your legs are powerful! I should call you SUPER BEE!"

$$300 \times 80 = 24,000$$

Hummy buzzed with pride, and Josh exclaimed, "Your wings must be strong, too. Hey! I can see through them!"

"Yes, my young friend. That's because they are **transparent**. You will also notice that they have long cells, like a leaf," said Hummy.

"What else can you tell me about your wings?" Josh questioned.

"Well, I have two pairs of wings, and the front wings are bigger than the back ones. My wings beat 250 times

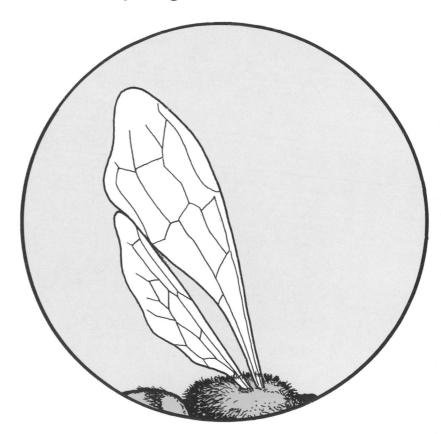

a second. That's why I buzz. My wings can also move in different ways, depending upon the job I'm doing. Sometimes my wings move in circles. Other times they move up and down. I was created perfectly for the many jobs I have to do.

Hummy began to show Josh her skill and speed as she called,
"I can hover,

climb,

dart,

stop,

swing

side to side . . .

hang upside down . . .

and

Z-O—O—-M!"

Hummy swooped around Josh so many times that his head began to whirl. "Hey! Slow down, you little insect acrobat!" he laughed.

As Josh stood up to stretch, Hummy came to rest on his shoulder. Josh walked along and thought about what he had learned.

Chapter 5

An Inside Look at the Honey Maker

"Let's see," Josh pondered. "Your head has your brain, mouth, tongue, antennae, and eyes. Your legs and wings are attached to your thorax, and you breathe through the spiracles in your abdomen. Is your stomach there, too?"

"In my abdomen I have a **honey-stomach** where I store the **nectar** that I sip from flowers. Some special chemicals begin to change the nectar into honey while it is still in my honey-stomach."

"Wow!" Josh exclaimed. "I can see that God really has a special plan for you."

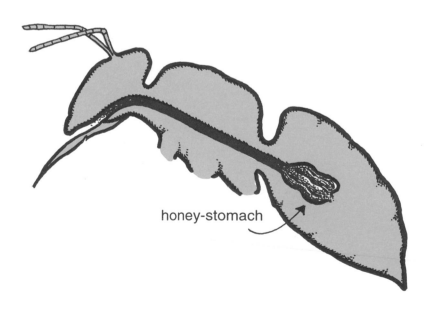

honey-stomach

"Ouch!" Josh howled suddenly.

"What happened?" Hummy asked.

"I just pricked my finger. I'll hold it against my shirt to keep it from bleeding. Do bees have blood, Hummy?"

"Yes, but we don't have red blood cells like you do. Our blood has no color. It is pumped forward from the heart and comes back to the thorax and abdomen. Then it goes again to the heart."

"What does your heart look like?" Josh wanted to know. "Is it in your thorax or abdomen?"

"My heart is a muscular tube in my abdomen," answered Hummy.

"Hummy, I've learned so much this morning," said Josh, "and it makes me want to learn more. It's a good thing Mom promised to take me to the library this afternoon. I think I'll pick up a book about honeybees at the library."

"My, it sounds like you're going to be busy. And this worker bee needs to get busy, too, doing the work I was meant to do. Bye!"

"May I meet you here again tomorrow, Hummy?" Josh asked.

But Hummy had already joined her friends at the hive, and Josh wasn't able to hear her reply.

He quickly gathered his things and ran home across the field.

"Bye!" he called. "And thanks!"

Chapter 6

Time to Ponder

When Josh returned home from the beehive, his mother and sister were ready to head into town.

Later, Josh was excited about all of the books he found about bees at the library. He even found stories about bees that he could share with his little sister. He

NO SMOKIN

enjoyed reading to Carrie, and he knew his Mother and sister both appreciated it, too.

That evening the family gathered at the dinner table, and Josh told his father about his day.

"Dad, do you remember where we saw the beehive on the other side of the field? Today I went out there and watched the bees. One bee came close to me and I studied it with my magnifying glass. Then Mom, Carrie, and I went to the library this afternoon. I checked out books on bees, and I plan to write down some of the things that I've learned—you know, the way scientists do. I made a list of things I still want to know. Tomorrow, I'm going back to talk to . . . I mean . . . to watch the bees again and see if I can find out more. . . ."

"Hey, hey! Slow down, son. It sounds like you've been as busy as a bee," Dad chuckled, as he picked up little Carrie.

"Daddy, Josh shared his books with me already, and he's going to read to me tonight, too," Carrie announced.

Their father smiled, "Say, that's good, for both of you!"

After dinner, Josh read another book to Carrie until it was time for bed. Josh's last waking thoughts before sleep were of pollen baskets and bees and honey and Hummy.

Chapter 7

Stings and Other Things

The next morning Josh quickly ate breakfast, politely asked to be excused, rushed outside and ran across the clover field. When he arrived at the oak tree, a bee had just landed on a clover blossom near the tree. Josh looked closely. Was it was Hummy? Yes!

"Good morning, my friend," Hummy buzzed.

"Oh, Hummy, I'm so glad to see you! I have a lot of questions to ask you. Last night I read that not all bees sting! Is that right?" Josh asked.

"Yes, that's true, Josh. Drones do not sting because they have no stingers. A young queen will sting another queen inside the hive if it tries to take her place. But we worker bees do not fight in the hive. We save our stings for people and animals who bother us."

Josh looked worried. "I hope I'm not bothering you," he exclaimed.

"It's okay," Hummy buzzed, "I mainly sting if an enemy tries to harm the hive."

"That's why beekeepers need to be so careful when they take honey from a hive, isn't it?" Josh asked.

"You're right, Josh. Most beekeepers use a type of smoke to control the bees while they take the honey. Smoke makes us bees fill up with honey. When we are full of honey, we are in a good mood. A good beekeeper will use only a small amount of smoke, and he doesn't take all of our honey. He always leaves enough for the bees to live on. He will not ruin our hive! Remember though, Josh, I will sting if I am hurt or if someone scares me."

"Hummy," Josh asked, "what happens when a bee does sting a person?"

"The bee dies," Hummy answered sadly, "because she loses her stinger and parts of her body in the person's skin."

"How sad! The bee loses her life, trying to save another! I know that I will be careful not to bother you or your friends while you are working. I will also tell my friends to be kind to bees!" said Josh. "I know now that drones don't sting. What more can you tell me about them?"

"Drones buzz and tumble all around. They may seem noisy and they don't work as hard as workers, but we couldn't get along without them."

"Do drones collect nectar like you do?" Josh asked.

"No, they don't. Their mouths aren't shaped for that. They don't get pollen and they don't have pollen baskets on their legs. They don't help to build the hive, either."

"Well, then, what do the drones do?" Josh wanted to know.

"Drones have one very special job to do. Drones mate with the queen bee, who then becomes the mother of the baby bees," Hummy said.

"You're right, Hummy. Drones are important too. I am beginning to see how God's plan for honeybees works. He created all of you with a special job to do, didn't He?"

Hummy buzzed happily in agreement.

Josh continued, "I'm beginning to see why people say 'busy as a bee.' You workers sure do a lot! Let's see, you find flowers, sip nectar, gather pollen, make honey, and guard the hive."

"Yes," said Hummy, "and we help to care for the queen and the wax castle!"

Chapter 8

The Queen and Her Castle

"Wax castle?" Josh looked confused. "What's a **wax castle**?"

"There's a wax castle right up here. Wax castles are beehives. One of the jobs of a worker bee is to build the wax castle," answered Hummy. "While the queen is laying eggs, the workers follow her. They feed her and keep her clean.

"Workers also clean the cells of the hive and feed the babies special food. Workers serve as guards of the hive."

"Do you workers each do all of those jobs every day?" asked Josh in amazement.

"No," Hummy laughed. "You may think I'm a superbee, but I don't do it all in one day!. Worker bees do each job at a different period in their lives."

"Last night I read that worker bees and the queen bee come from eggs that look alike."

"That is true, Josh. But the queen is fed different food, and she grows up in a larger space in the castle."

"The queen's body is longer than yours," Josh remembered.

"Yes," Hummy replied. "And her body is beautiful. The queen's only job is to lay eggs. She is the mother of all the baby bees. Listen to this! A young queen in a strong colony may lay 200,000 or more eggs a year. Since the queen may live up to five years, she might lay as many as one million eggs."

"Wow! I can hardly believe it!" Josh crowed. Then he looked up to the tree. "I'd like to see the inside of the hive. Do you think I could?"

"Okay! First, let me explain what I am doing here in the field. Then I'll take you back to the hive and you can meet some of my friends," Hummy suggested.

"I'd like that, Hummy!" Josh said. He followed Hummy to an especially lovely clover blossom.

"When you look at a flower, it's easy to notice its colorful petals. Birds and insects, especially honeybees, are attracted to a flower by its color and its fragrance, or smell. Some flowers have a sweet, juicy nectar that is delicious to drink. Some flowers produce a lot of powdery pollen.

"I'm collecting **pollen** today and I'll use the pollen for food back at the hive. Sometimes I collect pollen when I am gathering nectar. When I bump into a flower **stamen**, powdery pollen flies all over my body. Sometimes I get slapped in the face with it!"

"Oo-oo! You must be a sight!" Josh squealed.

"I scrape off the sticky pollen with my front legs and jaws and store it in my pollen baskets."

Josh watched closely. "You're beginning to look fat, Hummy."

Hummy chuckled. "You'd look fat too, if you had picked up pollen from a thousand flowers!"

"Wow! 1,000 flowers!" Josh was surprised!

"I'll just fly to a few more flowers and then we will head back to the hive," hummed the bee.

"Are you sure you're not bothering the flowers?" Josh asked.

"No, in fact I'm doing the flowers a favor by **pollinating** them. When I carry pollen from flower to flower I am helping the flowers make seeds," said Hummy.

"Bees and flowers really work together. You bees get nectar from the flower's pollen for food, yet you help the flowers by carrying pollen from one flower to another of the same kind. Hummy how did everything work out so perfectly?"

"Do you remember that I told you about how perfect God's plan was when He created bees? Well, He planned for the flowers to be a part of this creation, too. Isn't it exciting to know that God thought of all of this?"

A few minutes later, Josh followed Hummy to the hive. He watched Hummy unload her pollen baskets. First, she lowered her back legs into a cell. Then she pushed off the balls of pollen with her middle pair of legs. Josh

watched another worker bee break up the lump of pollen
Hummy had left at the hive. The worker in the
hive—called a housebee—laid the pollen on the bottom of
a cell. Then she pounded it down with her head.

"What do bees use pollen and honey for?" Josh asked.
"Do they eat it like people do?"

"Yes, honey and pollen are food for bees. A good
beekeeper will feed his bees or plant crops around the
hives so the bees don't run out of honey. After a

beekeeper takes honey from a hive, there should be at least fifteen pounds of honey left in the hive for the bees to live on. C'mon. I'm going to get nectar now."

For a moment, Josh looked confused. "Hummy, aren't nectar and honey the same thing?"

"I'm glad you asked that question, Josh. They are not the same. Flowers make nectar, and bees use it to make honey."

"Oh, I remember now. You told me the other day that you stored nectar in your honey-stomach."

"That's right," Hummy said. She landed on a flower. She let down her long tongue-tube to suck up some nectar. "I'm glad I found such a good supply of nectar so close to the hive today. Yesterday I flew two miles from the hive to find enough nectar."

"Hummy, do you use your sky map when you return to the hive after traveling so far?"

"Yes, I do, and I have never gotten lost," Hummy said. "I do have a friend, though, who entered the wrong hive. The bees in that hive let her in because she was full of nectar. That doesn't happen very often though. Usually a strange bee is treated as an enemy."

When Hummy returned to the hive, Josh watched as she brought up some of the nectar from her stomach. The nectar was mixed with juices from the bee. The other bees in the hive worked with it as it got thicker and thicker. Then they put it into a cell and held it in place with a wax cap. In the cell, the juices from the bee continued to work to change the nectar into honey. Only

God knows exactly how the bees make honey, and He designed only the bee to do this special job!

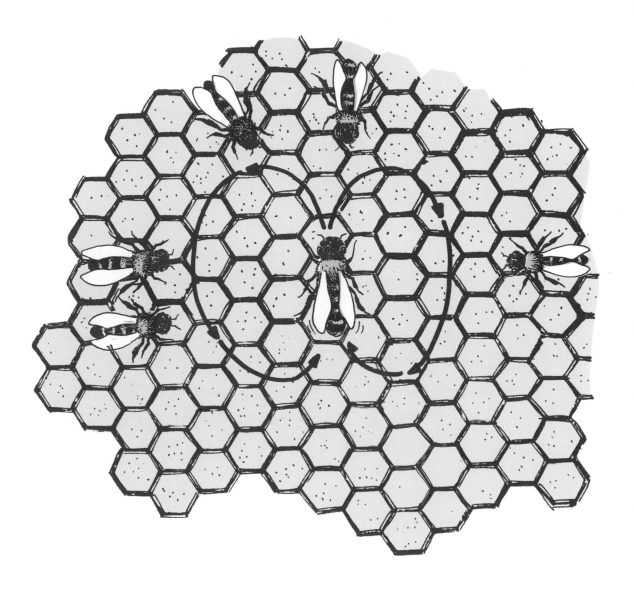

Hummy buzzed back to Josh. "Worker bees like to work together. When I find a good supply of nectar all by myself, I go back and tell the other workers."

"How do you tell them?"

"I do a special dance. Would you like to watch me, Josh?"

"Sure!" Josh replied.

Hummy flew to the hive. When she saw another worker bee, she circled one way and then another. In between the circles, she walked a straight line. Then she wiggled more. As other bees came out of the hive, they followed the dance. They did just what Hummy did. Then they left the hive and went to the find the nectar.

Hummy flew past Josh and buzzed, "I need to join the others now. Bye!"

"Okay, Hummy! I'll see you tomorrow!" Josh called.

At home that night Josh read more about the dance of the bees. This is what he found out. The dance tells how far away the flowers are. The farther away the nectar flowers are, the more circles the bee dances. The straight line points the direction to travel. Also, The fragrance of the flowers clings to the bee's body. It tells what kind of flowers they will find. When the bee finishes her dance, the other bees can tell exactly how far and where to go to find the nectar!

Josh fell asleep dreaming about the dance of the bees. He also dreamed about how wise God was to plan all of this!

Chapter 9

Wax Castles

In the morning Josh had to clean his room before he went to the beehive. He decided to do a neat job, like bees do, so he wouldn't have to waste time by having to do it again. His mother was thrilled with his work, and she hugged him as he headed out the door.

Hummy flew out of the hive as Josh ran across the field.

"Hi there, Josh. I'm glad you came. I want to show you more of the wax castles today! Come and see!"

Josh heard loud humming. He came as close as he could and carefully peeked into the beehive's opening. There he saw heavy curtains of wax hanging from the ceiling of the hive.

Josh saw many honeybees on both sides of the wax curtains. The bees were poking their heads into thousands of tiny rooms. These little chambers were the wax cells.

"What are they doing?" Josh asked.

"Those bees are cleaning the castle," Hummy buzzed.

"Why are these other bees beating their wings so fast?" Josh asked.

"Those bees are keeping the hive cool. If the temperature gets too warm, the honeycombs will melt," Hummy explained.

---

*Parent Note: Please caution children never to disturb a real beehive.

"Hey! Your hive has its own air conditioner!" Josh cried.

"Yes. That's a good way to describe it," Hummy laughed.

"What do bees do in the winter time, Hummy? How do they keep the hive warm when it is cold outside?"

"In the winter the bees eat a lot of honey to have the energy they need to stay warm," Hummy answered. Many bees move closer together, and make a blanket with their bodies. They move their wings to keep warm, much like people shiver and rub their arms on a cold day. When the bees near the outside get too cold, other bees trade places with them."

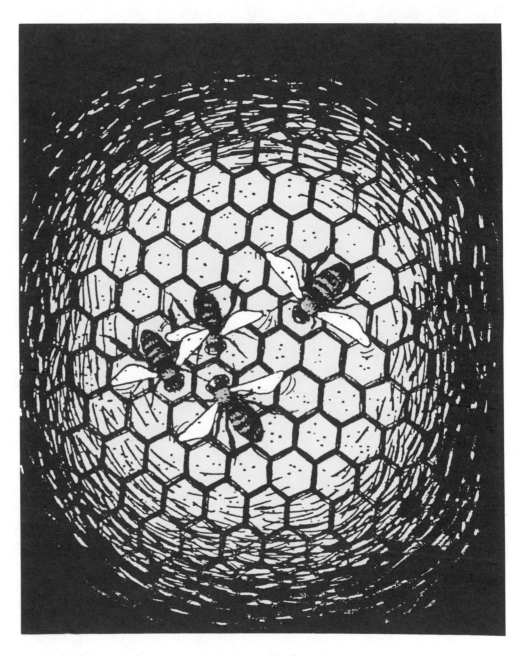

"You sure know how to work together!" Josh smiled.
Then he pointed to some cells. "I see these little rooms all
over the castle. How do you build them?"

"The bees use something called beeswax, which is
made by **glands** in the **abdomen** of each bee." Hummy
went on to explain. "Each worker has wax pockets on the
underside of her abdomen. She uses her legs to move the

wax from her pockets to her mouth. Then she chews and chews on the wax. Each bee adds her bit of wax and molds it into place. The next worker does the same. Each small room, or cell, is built by many bees."

"The walls look strong, and each cell has six sides!" Josh exclaimed.

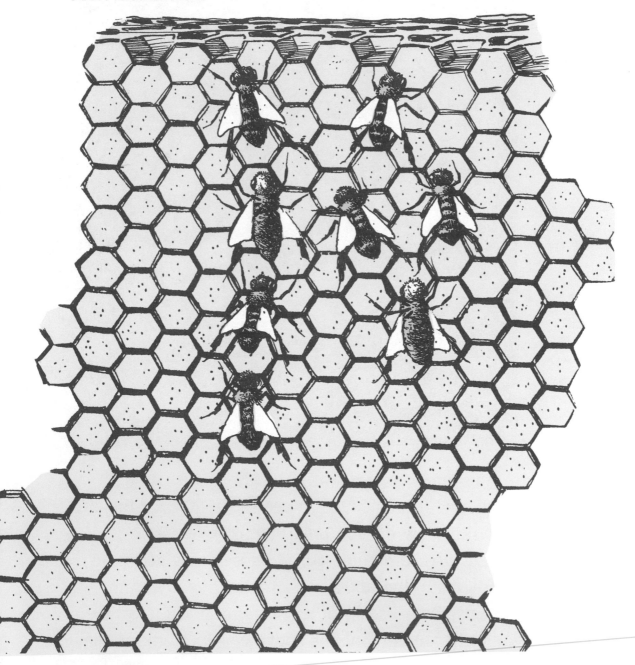

"Yes, Josh. God knew that this shape would make the honeycomb very strong. The honeycomb is straight. The outside edge is high to keep the honey and baby bees safe inside."

"How long will a honeycomb last?" Josh asked.

Upper layer of honeycomb (Unfilled)

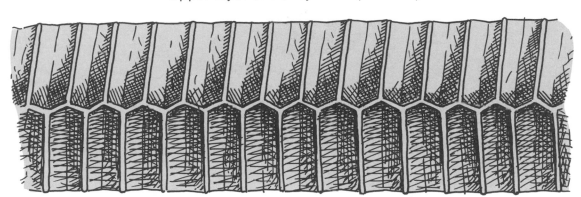

Lower layer of honeycomb (Filled)

"Honeycombs are so well made that they can be used again and again for 20 or 30 years."

"That's a LONG TIME!" Josh was surprised!

Hummy continued, "The bees build the rooms to be used in different ways. Extra-large cells are made for the eggs that will become queen bees. Drones' cells are also large and are found along the outside edge of the comb. The cells for the worker bees are small."

"No wonder you call your home a wax castle!" Josh said excitedly. "It is made of wax. It has a lovely design. It is very strong and can last a long time. It is built by many workers, and there are many rooms. Some rooms are small and some are big. It must be a grand thing to live in such a castle!"

Chapter 10

And Life Goes On

"Yes, the hive is a perfect place for bees to live," Hummy agreed.

Suddenly Josh asked, "When will all of these rooms be used?"

Hummy continued, "The queen will soon walk over the empty honeycomb, searching for clean, empty cells. Worker bees clean out the cells that other workers were hatched from. Worker cells are used over and over again to raise a new **generation** of bees."

Josh pointed out, "That's great! Even bees know how to recycle."

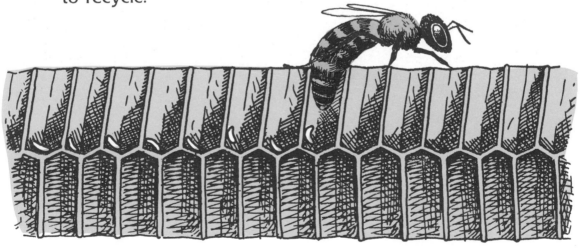

Hummy laughed, "You could say that. Reusing the old cells saves a lot of time and energy. The queen even knows which kind of egg to lay in each cell."

"When will the eggs hatch?" Josh asked.

"In about three days, each egg hatches into a **larva**. The workers feed all honeybee **larvae** a special milk-white **brood** food called **royal jelly** for the first three days. On the fourth day, drone and worker larvae are switched to a **diet** of **beebread**. Beebread is pollen mixed with nectar or watered-down honey. The larva of the queen continues to be fed royal jelly."

"Do they get fed like this until they're grown up?"

"No, Josh. After many days, the workers put a plug of

wax over each cell. The larva rests. At this stage, it is called the **pupa**. Now, many changes take place. At the proper time, the full-grown bee eats its way out of the cell."

"Do all of the bees come out of their cells on the same day?"

"No, the queen comes out on the sixteenth day. On the twenty-first day after the egg was laid, the worker bites her way out of the cell. The drone finds his way out of his cell on the twenty-fourth day after the egg was laid."

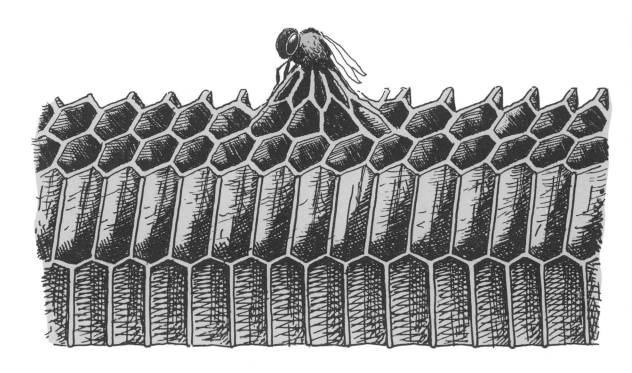

"What do the new bees do then?" Josh wondered.

"As each bee comes out of its cell, it will ask for food from a passing worker. From then on, each bee feeds itself. The queen will be fed again by the workers after she has mated with the drones."

"Hummy, what happens to the other new queen bees?" Josh wanted to know.

Hummy sadly explained. "Unfortunately, the first young queen who comes out of her cell will probably try to kill the other queen bees. It is also possible that the workers will finish the job she begins. From now on, the life of the castle centers around the queen bee. She lives the longest. Only the queen can lay eggs."

"All the bees sure do work hard for their queen bee," Josh thought aloud.

Hummy said, "Creation scientists believe that the queen bee was specially designed by our intelligent Creator from the beginning just to be able to lay eggs."

Then she suddenly warned, "Stand back, Josh! Watch what's happening!"

The queen and many drones flew from the hive. Drones from other hives met them in the sky.

"What's happening, Hummy?"

"The queen is ready to lay eggs. She is leaving the hive to meet with the drones. She will mate with the fastest and strongest drones," explained Hummy.

"Hummy, what happens to the drones?"

"They die right after they mate," said Hummy, "for they have finished the job they were designed to do."

"O-h-h-h," Josh said sadly. "Then what happens?"

"Josh, my story is nearly finished. When the queen returns to her castle, she settles down. Once she begins laying eggs, she never leaves the hive again, unless it becomes too crowded. If this should happen, the queen and many of the workers will fly away and set up a new castle. She only does this after the new queen has been raised. The old queen leaves, and the new queen stays."

Josh noticed that Hummy seemed kind of tired. "What will you do now, Hummy?" he asked.

"I will not live much longer. I am getting old. Young workers are hatching. They will take my place."

Josh felt a lump grow in his throat. He knew that a bee's life was very short, but he was going to miss his little friend.

Hummy seemed to understand. She softly buzzed, "Josh, I know you won't forget me. Remember that you

will be able to come and watch my sisters and brothers as they work around the hive."

"Oh, Hummy, I will miss you! You're right, I will never forget you. Thank you for all you have taught me. Now I have a better understanding about why you were created so wonderfully."

Josh sadly waved to his friend as she flew back to the hive. He called to her, "Hummy, I think you're WONDERFUL! God must have thought you were special, too. He created you and your friends so marvelously."

Josh smiled as he walked home. These had been good days with Hummy. He realized that bees are very special in God's eyes! They build fine castles, talk by doing a dance, air condition their homes, and protect their little ones. Nothing else can do all the things little bees do. They make royal jelly, beebread, and honey, one of the purest foods known. "I wonder if Hummy knows that the Bible talks about her?" He thought about some verses he had read.

"My son, eat thou honey, because it is good; and the honeycomb, which is sweet to thy taste" (Proverbs 24:13).

". . . sweeter also than honey and the honeycomb" (Psalm 19:10).

". . . and behold there was a swarm of bees and honey. . . . And he took thereof in his hands, and went on eating. . ." (Judges 14:8–9).

"And God saw every thing that He had made, and, behold, it was very good" (Genesis 1:31).

Josh was glad he had met Hummy. He enjoyed learning more about the world God had made. As Josh wandered homeward, he kicked a loose stone into some grass. A frightened field mouse scurried past an ant hill, and a huge, shiny black beetle hid under a piece of rotting wood. A distant bird warbled a happy call, and Josh suddenly realized that although his time with Hummy had ended, his summer adventures had just begun. Which of God's creatures would he choose to study next?

Which would *you* choose?

Bibliography

Books:

Cole, Joanna, *The Magic School Bus Inside a Beehive*, Scholastic, New York, 1996.

Farb, Peter, *The Insects*, Life's Nature Library, Time, Inc., New York, 1962.

Fischer-Nagel, Heiderose and Andreas, *Life of the Honeybee*, Carolrhoda Books, Minneapolis, 1986.

Frisch, Karl von, *Dance Language and Orientation of Bees*, Belknap Press, Cambridge, Mass., 1967.

Gould, James L., *The Honey Bee*, Scientific American Library, New York, 1995.

Hogan, Paula Z., *The Honeybee*, Raintree Steck-Vaughan Publishers, Milwaukee, Wisc., 1991.

Hornblow, Lenora and Arthur, *Insects Do the Strangest Things*, Step-Up-Books, Random House, New York, 1968.

Hubbell, Sue, *A Book of Bees; and How to Keep Them*, Random House, New York, 1988.

Johnson, Sylvia A., *A Beekeeper's Year*, Little, Brown, Boston, 1994.

Julivert, Angels, *The Fascinating World of Bees*, Barron's, New York, 1991.

Kelsy, Elim, *Bees*, Grolier, Danbury, Conn., 1986.

Kerby, Mona, *Friendly Bees, Ferocious Bees*, F. Watts, New York, 1987.

Lecht, Jane, *Honeybees*, National Geographic Society, Washington, D.C., 1973.

Michener, Charles D., *The Social Behavior of the Bees*, The Belknap Press of Harvard University Press, Cambridge, 1974.

More, Daphne, *The Bee Book: The History and Natural History of the Honeybee*, Universe Books, New York, 1976.

Parker, Steve, *Insects: How to Watch and Understand the Busy World of Insects*, Eyewitness Explorers Series, Doris Kindersley, Inc., New York, 1992.

Rood, Ronald, *It's Going to Sting Me*, Simon and Schuster, New York, 1976.

Rowan, James P., *Honeybees*, Rourke Corporation, Vero Beach, Fla., 1993.

Tompkins, Enoch H., and Roger Griffith, *Practical Beekeeping*, Garden-Way Publishing, Charlotte, 1977.

Winston, Mark L., *The Biology of the Honey Bee*, Harvard University Press, Cambridge, Mass., 1987.

Chart:

Bee Chart, The Walter T. Kelly Co., Darkson, Kentucky, 42726. (This chart may be ordered for classroom use.)

Glossary

Abdomen (ab´duh muhn) The third part of the bee; it contains the heart, stomachs and breathing holes

Antennae (an ten´e) The feelers which are found on the head of the bee

Beebread (be´bred) Food fed to the very young forms of the drone and worker bees; it is made of pollen and nectar (these words defined below)

Brood (brüd) A group of young bees

Chemical (kem´uh kuhl) Simple materials that can be combined to make different materials

Complex (kom´pleks) Made up of many parts

Diet (di´uht) Food or drink that a person or animal usually takes

DNA A code that tells the cell what it is going to be

Drone (dron) The male bee, larger than a worker

Generation (jen e ra´shuhn) The period of time between one succession of bees and the next.

Gland (gland) Part of the body which makes and gives out materials

Hinge (hinj) A movable place where two things or parts are joined together

Honey-stomach (hun´e stum´uhk) Part of the food tube of the bee that produces chemicals that change the nectar into honey; it stores nectar until the bee returns to the hive.

Larva (lär´vuh) Early, wormlike form of a bee from the time it leaves the egg until it reaches the second stage; **Larvae** means more than one larva

Lens (lenz) Part of the eye that focuses light; **Lenses** means more than one

Muscles (mus´uhlz) Parts in the bodies of bees that can be tightened or loosened to make the body move

Nectar (nek´tuhr) Sweet liquid found in many flowers

Nerve (nérv) Long cell that carries messages to and from the brain

Pollen (pol´uhn) Fine powder or dust formed by a flower; necessary to make seeds

Pollen Baskets (pol´uhn bas´kits) Pouches used to carry pollen; they are found on the back legs of the worker bee

Pollinating (pol´uhn nat ing) Scattering pollen

Pupa (pyu´puh) A bee in its third stage of growth when it is sealed inside a cell

Royal Jelly (roil jel´e) A creamy food, full of special vitamins, that is fed to queen bee larvae

Queen Bee (kwen be) Large female bee which lays eggs

Spiracles (spi´ruh kuhlz) Breathing holes in the bee's abdomen

Stamen (sta´muhn) The part of the flower that holds the pollen

Thorax (thôr´aks) The middle part of the bee; the bee's "motor room;" wings and legs are attached to the thorax

Transparent (trans par´uhnt) Clear enough to see through

Ultraviolet Rays (ul truh vi´uh lit raz) Special rays that can be seen by bees but not by people

Vibrations (vi bra´shuhnz) Rapid back-and-forth motions

Wax Castle (waks kas´uhl) A beehive

Worker Bee (wér´kuhr be) Female bee that gathers pollen and nectar; she cares for the queen and the babies; she builds the wax castles